MY LITTLE SISTER ATE ONE HARE

by Bill Grossman • illustrated by Kevin Hawkes

 Dragonfly Books™ • Crown Publishers, Inc. • New York

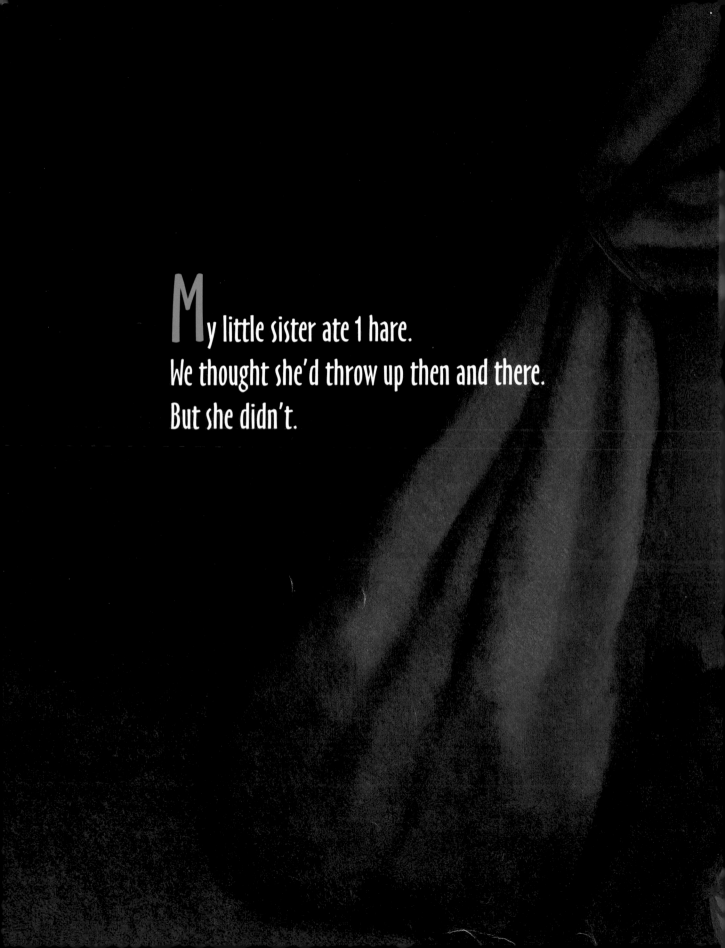

My little sister ate 1 hare.
We thought she'd throw up then and there.
But she didn't.

My little sister ate 2 snakes.
She ate 2 snakes, for heaven sakes!
She ate 2 snakes. She ate 1 hare.
We thought she'd throw up then and there.
But she didn't.

My little sister ate 3 ants.
She even ate their underpants.
She ate 2 snakes. She ate 1 hare.
We thought she'd throw up then and there.
But she didn't.

My little sister ate 4 shrews.
She ate their smelly socks and shoes.
She ate 3 ants, 2 snakes, 1 hare.
We thought she'd throw up then and there.
But she didn't.

My little sister ate 5 bats.
She ate their coats and ties and hats.
4 shrews, 3 ants, 2 snakes, 1 hare.
We thought she'd throw up then and the
But she didn't.

My little sister ate 6 mice,
Then spit them out and ate them twice.
She ate 5 bats, 4 shrews, 3 ants.
She even ate their underpants.
She ate 2 snakes. She ate 1 hare.
We thought she'd throw up then and there.
But she didn't.

She captured 7 polliwogs
And ate them as they turned to frogs.
She ate 6 mice, 5 bats, 4 shrews.
She ate their smelly socks and shoes.
She ate 3 ants, 2 snakes, 1 hare.
We thought she'd throw up then and there.
But she didn't.

My little sister ate 8 worms.
She ate those worms with all their germs.
She captured 7 polliwogs
And ate them as they turned to frogs.
She ate 6 mice. She ate 5 bats.
She ate their coats and ties and hats.
4 shrews, 3 ants, 2 snakes, 1 hare.
We thought she'd throw up then and there.
But she didn't.

My little sister ate 9 lizards.
She ate their heads and legs and gizzards.
My little sister ate 8 worms.
She ate those worms with all their germs.
And 7 polliwogs, 6 mice.
She spit them out and ate them twice.
5 bats, 4 shrews, 3 ants, 2 snakes.
She ate 2 snakes, for heaven sakes!
And, of course, she ate 1 hare.
We thought she'd throw up then and there.
But she didn't.

My little sister ate 10 peas.
But eating healthy foods like these
Makes my sister sick, I guess.

Oh, my goodness! What a mess!

To Evelyn and Mike Anischik
—B. G.

To Jessie, who entertains us all
—K. H.

DRAGONFLY BOOKS ™ PUBLISHED BY CROWN PUBLISHERS, INC.

Text copyright © 1996 by Bill Grossman
Illustrations copyright © 1996 by Kevin Hawkes

Published by Crown Publishers, Inc., a Random House company, 201 East 50th Street, New York, NY 10022

CROWN is a trademark of Crown Publishers, Inc.

http://www.randomhouse.com/

Library of Congress Cataloging-in-Publication Data
Grossman, Bill.
My little sister ate one hare / by Bill Grossman ; illustrated by Kevin Hawkes.
p.   cm.
Summary: Little sister has no problem eating one hare, two snakes, and three ants, but when she gets to ten peas, she throws up quite a mess.
[1. Counting. 2. Stories in rhyme.] I. Hawkes, Kevin, ill. II. Title.
PZ8.3.G914Mn   1996
[E] — dc20   95-7539

ISBN 0-517-59600-8 (trade)
ISBN 0-517-59601-6 (lib. bdg.)
ISBN 0-517-88576-X (pbk.)

First Dragonfly Books ™ edition: September 1998

Printed in the U.S.A.

10 9 8 7

DRAGONFLY BOOKS is a trademark of Alfred A. Knopf, Inc.